Thomas the Tank Engine & Friends **A BRITT ALLCROFT COMPANY PRODUCTION** Based on The Railway Series by the Rev W Awdry. Copyright © Gullane (Thomas) LLC 1999. All rights reserved under International and Pan-American Copyright Conventions. Published in the United States by Random House, Inc., New York, and simultaneously in Canada by Random House of Canada Limited, Toronto.
Illustrated by Tommy Stubbs

www.randomhouse.com/kids   www.thomasthetankengine.com

Library of Congress Cataloging-in-Publication Data
Thomas the really useful engine : based on The railway series by the Rev. W. Awdry. Summary: When a storm damages Tidmouth Station and all the other train engines are stranded, Thomas and his driver save the day.
ISBN 0-375-80242-8 (trade) — ISBN 0-375-90242-2 (lib. bdg.)
[1. Railroads—Trains—Fiction. 2. Storms—Fiction.] I. Stubbs, Tommy, ill. II. Awdry, W. Railway series.
PZ7.T3695 1999 [E]—dc21 98-53769

Printed in the United States of America   October 1999   10 9 8 7 6 5

RANDOM HOUSE and colophon are registered trademarks of Random House, Inc.

THOMAS
The Really Useful Engine

THOMAS
THE TANK ENGINE & FRIENDS

Random House 🏠 New York

Thomas was a little blue tank engine who lived on the Island of Sodor. He was a Really Useful Engine who had his very own branch line.

He had two coaches, Annie and Clarabel. "Hurry, hurry!" they would say to Thomas as he pulled them through the countryside.

Thomas had many engine friends. Gordon and Henry were big, Edward and Percy were small, and James was somewhere in between. Sir Topham Hatt was the director of the railway. He was fond of all the engines—even though they sometimes made trouble for him.

One day, there was a terrible storm. Thunder rolled and lightning flashed and rain fell heavily all over the island.

A fierce wind rocked the boats in the harbor…

…and knocked down trees in the forest.

The engines sat in their shed at the station, looking out at the storm. Henry the Green Engine did not like storms. He closed his eyes and hoped it would end soon.

Suddenly, a strong wind blew, and a tall tree fell onto the station house's roof! *Crash!*

"Oh, dear!" said Henry with a shudder.

Sir Topham Hatt came at once to inspect the damage. Luckily, no one was hurt.

"This roof must be repaired as soon as possible," Sir Topham announced. He put Gordon the Big Express Engine in charge.

Gordon was quite pleased. "After all," he boasted, "I *am* the biggest, the fastest, and the strongest."

James the Red Engine was annoyed. He wished that he were the one in charge. "*I'm* the one who's used to pulling freight cars," he grumbled.

"Off you go, then!" Gordon ordered James. "Fetch us some lumber and bricks and new slate!"

The rain started again. It began falling into the station house! The train crew set out buckets so people waiting for trains wouldn't get wet.

Everyone waited for James to return. The roof continued to leak. So the stationmaster invited passengers to use his parlor as a waiting room.

"Henry and Percy, go see what's taking James so long," Gordon ordered.

Percy the Small Engine was eager to go. But Henry puffed off slowly. He did not like being wet at all!

Now everyone waited for James, Henry, and Percy to return. Sir Topham Hatt was busy checking on the railway. "Are all the train lines cleared for travel?" he asked the stationmaster.

Thomas was getting worried. Maybe the other engines were stuck somewhere!

"We've got to help," Thomas said to his driver.

His driver nodded. "Well, you *do* know your way around the island," he admitted to Thomas. "Let's go!"

Full of steam, Thomas puffed out of the yard and down the tracks. *"Peep, peep!"* he whistled.

"Gordon wanted lumber, so James must have gone to get some," said Thomas.

"First stop—the forest!" his driver said.

When they arrived in the forest, they didn't see James. But there was Henry, who had run out of steam and broken down!

"I knew I shouldn't have gone out in this frightful weather," Henry said, coughing.

Thomas' driver helped Henry's driver call for assistance. Then Thomas continued on his way. He was worried about Percy and James. *"Peep, peep!"* he whistled, puffing along. "Gordon also wanted bricks," he remembered.

"Next stop—the clay pits!" said his driver.

When they arrived at the clay pits, they didn't see James. But there was Percy, stuck behind a large tree that had fallen across the tracks!

"I'm just too little!" cried Percy.

"Even Gordon wouldn't be able to cross that," Thomas said kindly. His driver called for a breakdown train to help clear Percy's rails.

Then Thomas continued on his way. He was still worried about James.

"*Peep, peep!* Gordon also wanted slate," Thomas said to his driver.

"Next stop—the quarry!" said the driver.

When they got to the quarry, who should they spot but James. He was lying in mud on the side of the tracks!

"Oh, oh!" James groaned. "Those horrible freight cars are nothing but trouble. They pushed me right off the rails! Then they ran away."

The rain had stopped by now, and Thomas heard a *whir* from above.

There was his pal Harold the Helicopter flying overhead!

"I've spotted James' freight cars!" Harold called. "They're down at the harbor."

Then Thomas heard another sound.

"Poop, poop!" Gordon was steaming around the bend.

"I'll help James," Gordon said to Thomas. "You go get those freight cars!"

"Peep, peep!" Thomas headed for the harbor as quickly as he could.

He heard the naughty freight cars before he even saw them! Loaded with goods and laughing loudly, they were pushing and bumping one another.

"Come along at once!" Thomas called sternly to them.

The freight cars stopped laughing when they heard Thomas.
"We were just having fun," they said sulkily.
"There's a job to be done—and you're making everyone wait!"
Thomas said.
He made the freight cars get in line and pulled them up from
the harbor.

All the engines steamed back to the station. First came Henry, then Percy, and then Gordon.

Next came James, pulling the naughty freight cars who had caused so much trouble! The freight cars grumbled and mumbled as they carried the lumber, bricks, and slate.

Thomas puffed along proudly at the back of the group. And Harold the Helicopter flew above all of them.

Everyone was happy to see the missing engines. But there was no time to waste. The station still had to be repaired! Everyone pitched in and helped put up new beams, made of strong timber from the forest.

Crumbling bricks were replaced with new ones, made out of clay from the clay pits.

And the roof was patched with new pieces of slate from the quarry.

Soon the station house looked as good as new.

"We must have a Grand Gala to celebrate!" announced Sir Topham Hatt.

The conductors and engineers hung up banners and bunting. Even the engines looked festive!

The stationmaster passed around tea and cookies in the waiting room.

"Congratulations to all on a job well done!" said Sir Topham Hatt.

"Three cheers for Thomas! Hip, hip, hooray!" everyone called. "Thomas, you truly are a Really Useful Engine!"